The Time Traveller Book of VIKING RAIDERS

Anne Civardi and James Graham-Campbell

Illustrated by Stephen Cartwright
Designed by John Jamieson

Consultant: Dr. D. M. Wilson
Director of the British Museum

Contents

Going Back in Time

This book is for everyone who would like to travel back in time. You have probably tried to imagine how people used to live many years ago. Now we have invented a Magic Time Travelling Helmet to help you.

By putting on the Magic Helmet and pressing all the right buttons, you can go back to any time you want. This time you are going back over 1,000 years to Norway—the home of the Viking Raiders.

On the next page are the people you will meet on your trip. They are not real people. But the things they do are things real people have done. Below you can see how to work the Magic Time Travelling Helmet.

Put on the Helmet
Pick Your Destination

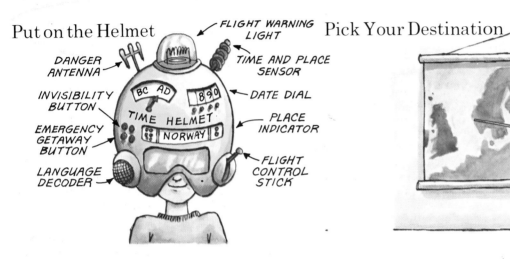

FLIGHT WARNING LIGHT

DANGER ANTENNA

TIME AND PLACE SENSOR

INVISIBILITY BUTTON

BC AD

890

DATE DIAL

TIME HELMET

EMERGENCY GETAWAY BUTTON

NORWAY

PLACE INDICATOR

LANGUAGE DECODER

FLIGHT CONTROL STICK

Here is your Magic Helmet. You can see it has many useful gadgets to help you travel back in time.

With it, your journey to visit the Vikings, more than ten centuries ago, only takes a few seconds.

You are almost ready. Set the place dial to 'southern Norway' and the date dial to '890 A.D.'.

Below are a few stop-offs you might pass on the way to give you an idea of how things change.

1940

Your first stop is in 1940, at about the time your parents were born.

Things have not changed very much, but notice the aeroplane and old radio.

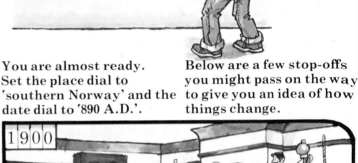

1900

Now a jump of 40 years—things have changed a lot. There are gas lamps, no

electricity, a funny telephone and a lot of decorated furniture.

1600

Back another 300 years—the room is lit by candles and heated by a log fire.

Notice the furniture and the small window with lots of tiny panes of glass.

1200

Now we are at the time when people live in big, cold castles. There is no

chimney for the fire, nor glass for the windows. Next stop—Norway.

The People You Will Meet

It is a hard life for the people you will meet in Norway. The winters are long and cold and it is difficult to grow good food. Most of the men are fierce warriors. In the summer, they sail across the sea to raid and loot other countries.

SVEN

EARL KNUT

ROLLO THE BLACKSMITH

Earl Knut is the most important chieftain in this part of Norway. He owns a lot of land which he farms with the help of his eldest son, Eric, and many slaves. Knut is very rich—he often goes raiding in Britain and Ireland to steal treasure and capture slaves. Although he is a fierce man, he is kind to his wife and children.

Astrid has been married to Knut for 24 years. When she was younger she went with him on his travels. Now, while he is away raiding, she stays at home and looks after the farm. Astrid is always busy spinning and weaving. She is a very good cook and brews strong beer.

ASTRID

Sven, the second son, is 21. He is wild and brave and enjoys going on raids with his father. One day he wants to be rich and famous too. He is also a trader and sells soapstone bowls, stolen treasure and slaves at the big trading towns down the coast.

Björn, the youngest son, is 19. His name means 'bear', but he is not really as strong and fierce as his brothers. Knut has given him a ship to take his family to settle in Iceland with some of their friends. Björn wants to find new land where he can have his own farm.

BJÖRN

Rollo, who is an old man now, comes from Rogaland in western Norway. He is the most important freeman on Earl Knut's farm. Rollo is a very skilled blacksmith and also makes fine jewellery. As well as weapons for the raiders, he makes farm tools, ship-building tools and pots and pans.

LEIF

Leif is learning to be a blacksmith and helps Rollo in the smithy. He has a very bad temper which often gets him into trouble.

COUSIN OLAF

Olaf, Earl Knut's first cousin, is also an important chieftain who owns a big farm and a longship for raiding. People call him Olaf Strongarm because he is famous for his great strength. When he was young, Olaf won many wrestling and weight-lifting competitions.

ERIC KNUTSSON

FREYDA

Freyda, the eldest daughter, is 16. Soon she will be married. Her mother is busy teaching her to cook, spin, weave and brew beer—all the things she needs to know to become a good wife. Freyda also helps to look after her two young sisters. There are no schools for them to go to—even their father cannot read or write.

Eric is 22 years old. Because he is the eldest son, he will take over his father's farm when he dies. Eric is called Knutsson, which means 'son of Knut'.

Many freemen work on Earl Knut's farm. They do not have their own land but the Earl has allowed them to build their own houses. In return, they help him to farm, build ships, smelt iron ore and carve soapstone.

FREEMEN

SLAVES

Slaves do all the dirtiest and nastiest work on the farm. At the moment, Knut has twelve slaves. But when he next goes raiding he will probably capture more. His slaves are never allowed to carry any weapons

3

Earl Knut's Farm

You have jumped back in time to the year 890 A.D. With the help of the Magic Helmet, you have landed on Earl Knut's farm on the shores of southern Norway. The long, cold winter is over and everybody is busy working on the land. There is lots to be done now that the snow has melted.

The Earl lives here with his wife Astrid, their six children and all their grandchildren. Astrid's aunt and her family live with them too.

Knut has many slaves and freemen to help him grow food, and to look after his cows, sheep and horses. All the slaves live together in a small, stone hut close to the main house, called the longhouse. The freemen have come from their houses on the Earl's land. Some of their wives and children help Astrid with the housework and cooking in Knut's longhouse.

These men are breaking up soapstone, a kind of soft rock, to make into bowls, lamps and fishing weights. Sven will take carved soapstone to sell when he goes trading down the coast.

OUTCROP OF SOAPSTONE

A herdsman drives the Earl's cows to higher pasture away from the farm where there is plenty of good grass. The cows will stay there the whole summer and get fat.

RUBBISH HEAP

VEGETABLE GARDEN

Rollo, the Blacksmith, spends all day in his workshop with his assistant, Leif. Here they make pots and pans, farm tools and weapons out of iron.

ROLLO'S WORKSHOP

THE LONG HOUSE

ROLLO GIVES ASTRID A NEW POT

WASHING CLOTHES

BATH HOUSE

Flax is growing in this field. Astrid will weave the flax into fine linen to make clothes for her family.

WOOL FROM THESE SHEEP WILL BE MADE INTO CLOTHES

A freeman ploughs a field to get it ready for sowing a crop of barley.

WOODEN PLOUGH

4

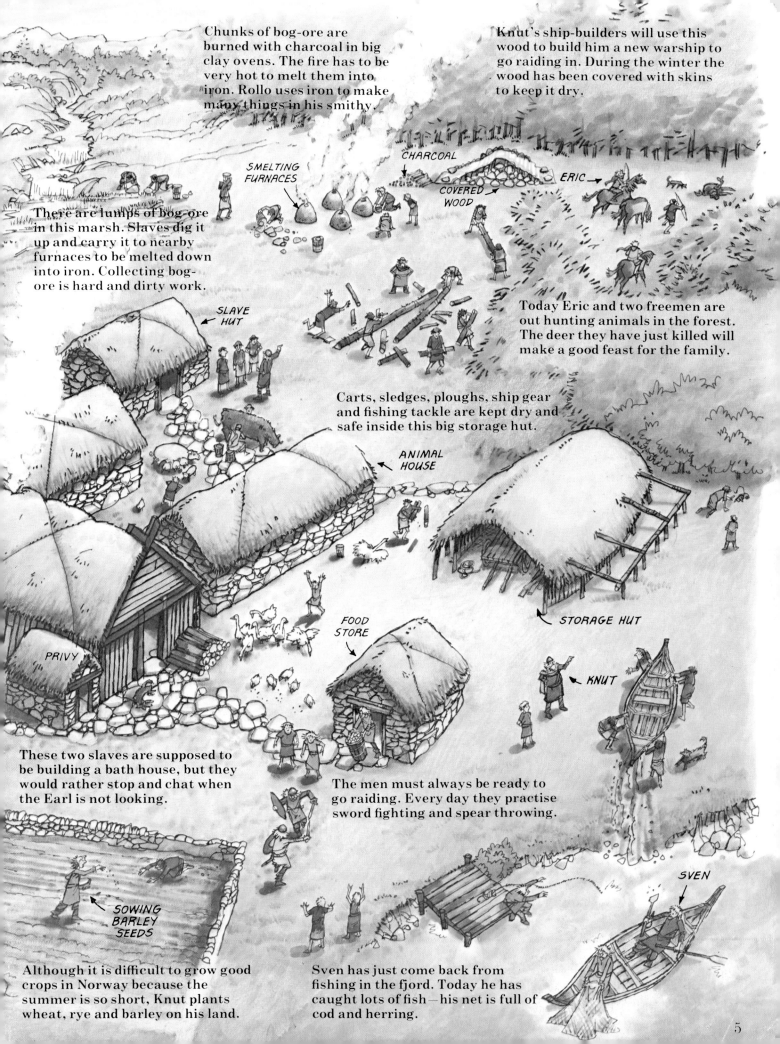

Chunks of bog-ore are burned with charcoal in big clay ovens. The fire has to be very hot to melt them into iron. Rollo uses iron to make many things in his smithy.

Knut's ship-builders will use this wood to build him a new warship to go raiding in. During the winter the wood has been covered with skins to keep it dry.

SMELTING FURNACES

CHARCOAL

COVERED WOOD

ERIC

There are lumps of bog-ore in this marsh. Slaves dig it up and carry it to nearby furnaces to be melted down into iron. Collecting bog-ore is hard and dirty work.

Today Eric and two freemen are out hunting animals in the forest. The deer they have just killed will make a good feast for the family.

SLAVE HUT

Carts, sledges, ploughs, ship gear and fishing tackle are kept dry and safe inside this big storage hut.

ANIMAL HOUSE

FOOD STORE

STORAGE HUT

KNUT

PRIVY

These two slaves are supposed to be building a bath house, but they would rather stop and chat when the Earl is not looking.

The men must always be ready to go raiding. Every day they practise sword fighting and spear throwing.

SOWING BARLEY SEEDS

SVEN

Although it is difficult to grow good crops in Norway because the summer is so short, Knut plants wheat, rye and barley on his land.

Sven has just come back from fishing in the fjord. Today he has caught lots of fish — his net is full of cod and herring.

5

Inside the Longhouse

Earl Knut and his family live together in the longhouse. The one big room is always dark, smoky and a bit smelly as there are no windows. A small hole in the roof lets out the smoke.

While he waits for his morning meal, the Earl is carving arrows. Astrid is weaving the last length of wool for the sail of his new ship. Eric is already out working on the farm.

At one end of the room, the women are busy preparing and cooking the food. Today, the family will eat hot barley and oat porridge, bread rolls, butter, cheese and milk.

Only Knut and Astrid have a proper bed to sleep in—everybody else lies on platforms. Knut's slaves sleep huddled together on the floor of their hut to keep warm.

There is very little furniture. The family keep all their things in big wooden chests.

BJÖRN

WOODEN CHEST

METAL OIL LAMP

SLAVE

SOUR MILK

FLOUR

SOAPSTONE OIL LAMP

How to Make Bread

1 QUERN — FLOUR — HOLE TO PUT IN GRAIN

The bread-maker grinds barley grain in a big quern made of stone. She turns the handle until the grain is ground into flour.

2 KNEADING DOUGH

Then she mixes the flour with water and kneads it together in a big wooden trough to make a dough.

3 METAL PAN

When the dough is properly mixed, the bread-maker shapes it into small loaves and bakes them over the hot ashes of the fire.

Making Wool into Thread

1 In early summer, Sven cuts the wool off the sheep with big, metal shears. Freyda washes the fleece in a stream and then hangs it up to dry.

2 To get rid of the knots and burrs, Freyda combs the wool over and over again with long metal-pronged combs. Now the wool is ready to be spun.

METAL COMB

3 She ties some wool to a stick. Then she spins the spindle and lets it drop. As it falls, still spinning, she pulls out more wool to make a thread.

SPINDLE
STICK CALLED DISTAFF
SOAPSTONE WEIGHT

4 Freyda takes the thread off the spindle and winds it round a yarn-winder. Sometimes she dyes the thread different colours with vegetable juices.

DYED THREAD

Eric's wife is beating flax to break it into short, thin threads. When she has enough, she will spin them into a long thread and give it to Astrid to weave into linen.

Freyda is very pleased with the ironing board Björn has made for her. He carved it out of whalebone. She smooths the clothes with a big, heated lump of glass.

The girls learn how to spin and weave when they are quite young. Astrid spends hours each day at her loom. From the cloth she weaves, she makes clothes, ship sails, blankets and wall hangings.

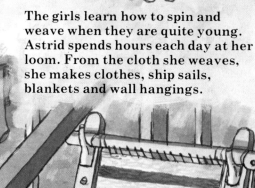

MALLET

FLAX

WHALEBONE BOARD

HOT PORRIDGE

SOAPSTONE LOOM WEIGHTS

BUTTER AND CHEESE

After a hard day's work on the farm, the men will be very hungry. Soon the women will start cooking the evening meal of meat, wild vegetables and fruit.

Most of the women wear big bronze brooches on their pinafore straps. Their sewing things—scissors, needles and tiny knives—hang on chains from the brooches.

Building a New Warship

For many weeks Earl Knut's freemen have been hard at work building a new warship. Carefully chosen trees from the forest were felled and left to dry long before the work began.

Knut has come to watch the carpenters rivet on the final planks—his ship is nearly ready. Soon he and his warriors will set off in the ship to spend the summer raiding.

The warship must be big and strong enough to cross the rough open sea to Ireland. It is about 24 metres long and 5 metres wide. There is room for 40 men to live on board.

Carpenters use adzes to shape a long, thick mast. The mast slots into a huge block of wood, shaped like a fish, in the middle of the warship's deck.

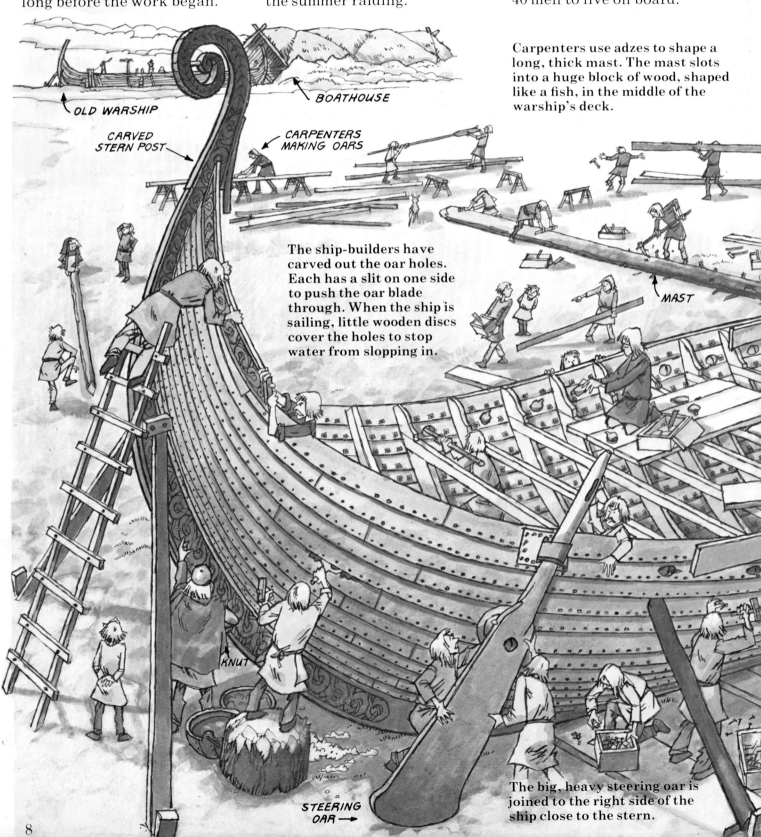

OLD WARSHIP

CARVED STERN POST

BOATHOUSE

CARPENTERS MAKING OARS

MAST

The ship-builders have carved out the oar holes. Each has a slit on one side to push the oar blade through. When the ship is sailing, little wooden discs cover the holes to stop water from slopping in.

KNUT

STEERING OAR

The big, heavy steering oar is joined to the right side of the ship close to the stern.

How a Ship is Built

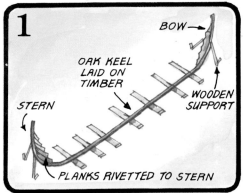

1

BOW

OAK KEEL LAID ON TIMBER

STERN

WOODEN SUPPORT

PLANKS RIVETTED TO STERN

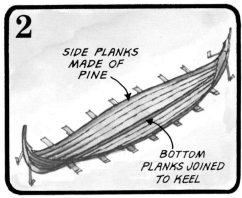

2

SIDE PLANKS MADE OF PINE

BOTTOM PLANKS JOINED TO KEEL

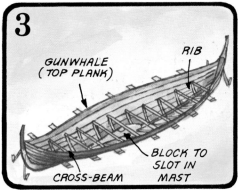

3

GUNWHALE (TOP PLANK)

RIB

CROSS-BEAM

BLOCK TO SLOT IN MAST

The trunk of a very tall oak tree is cut and shaped to make a strong, heavy keel. A curved piece of wood is joined to the front to make the bow. A second piece is joined to the back to make the stern.

The carpenters cut long planks out of pine trees. The pine planks, which make the ship light, are rivetted to the keel, bow and stern to form the bottom and the sides of the ship.

Then the ribs and cross-beams are fitted inside the ship. The planks are tied or rivetted to them. A huge block of wood is fixed into the bottom of the ship to hold up the heavy mast.

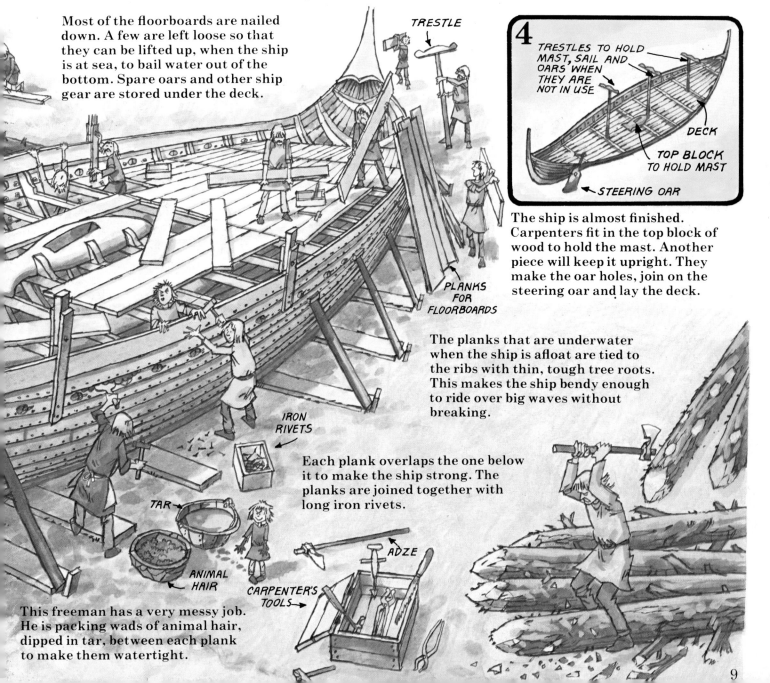

Most of the floorboards are nailed down. A few are left loose so that they can be lifted up, when the ship is at sea, to bail water out of the bottom. Spare oars and other ship gear are stored under the deck.

TRESTLE

PLANKS FOR FLOORBOARDS

IRON RIVETS

TAR

ANIMAL HAIR

CARPENTER'S TOOLS

ADZE

4

TRESTLES TO HOLD MAST, SAIL AND OARS WHEN THEY ARE NOT IN USE

DECK

TOP BLOCK TO HOLD MAST

STEERING OAR

The ship is almost finished. Carpenters fit in the top block of wood to hold the mast. Another piece will keep it upright. They make the oar holes, join on the steering oar and lay the deck.

The planks that are underwater when the ship is afloat are tied to the ribs with thin, tough tree roots. This makes the ship bendy enough to ride over big waves without breaking.

Each plank overlaps the one below it to make the ship strong. The planks are joined together with long iron rivets.

This freeman has a very messy job. He is packing wads of animal hair, dipped in tar, between each plank to make them watertight.

The Raiders Get Ready

At last Earl Knut's new ship is finished. Now he can go raiding. His three sons, Eric, Sven and Björn, and his most trusted freemen will go with him.

While they are away, the farm work must be done. Astrid is staying behind with five freemen and the slaves to help look after the farm.

Olaf, the Earl's cousin, has sailed down the coast to join him on the raids. Two other great chieftains and their warriors are going as well.

The Blacksmith's Workshop

Rollo is making and mending weapons for the raiders. His helper, Leif, keeps the charcoal fire glowing with big bellows. It makes him hot and bad-tempered.

When an iron bar is red hot, Rollo takes it off the fire with his tongs and beats it into shape on the anvil. He is making an axe as a present for Cousin Olaf.

Rollo decorates the axes, spears and swords he makes for chieftains with gold and silver. He may spend as long as a month working on a really special weapon.

Fighting Practice

The Vikings are very proud of being good fighters and owning fine weapons. Even young boys learn how to fight. Today is the last time for Knut and his men to practise before going on the raids.

Each man owns a sword, a spear, an axe and a shield—a few have bows and arrows. Some warriors have throwing spears which they hurl at the enemy, others have ones specially made for thrusting.

A Viking raider's most precious possession is his sword. With its sharp edges, it is a deadly weapon. Only great men, such as Knut and Olaf, wear coats of mail and metal helmets in battle.

10

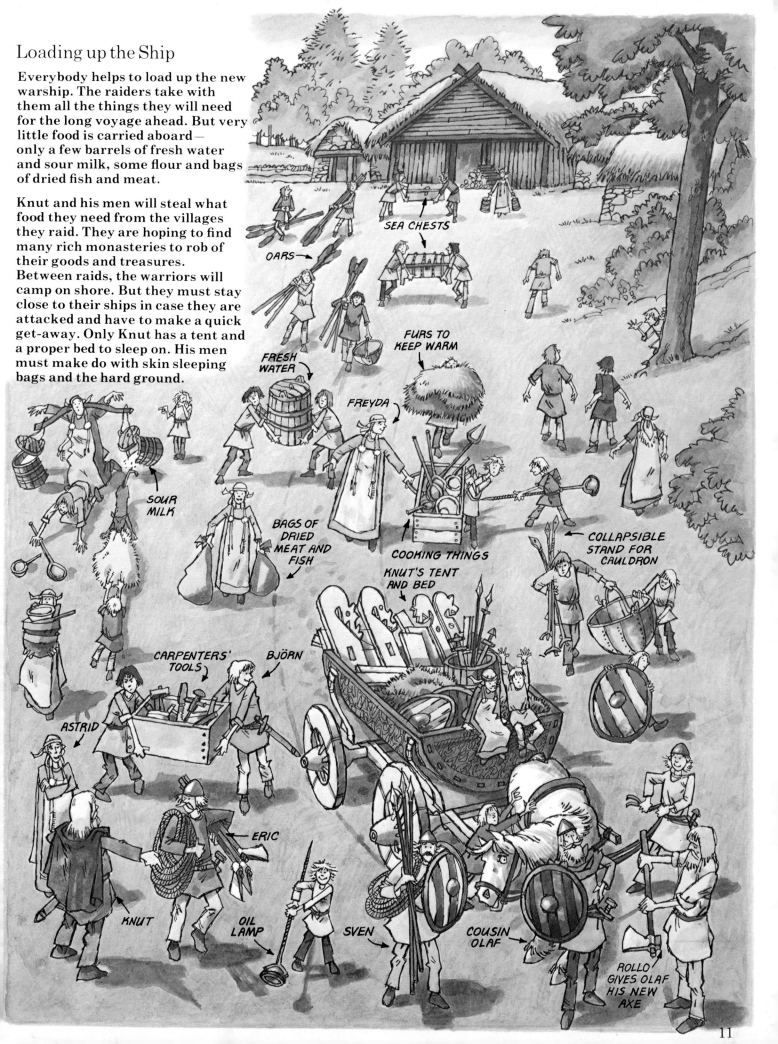

Loading up the Ship

Everybody helps to load up the new warship. The raiders take with them all the things they will need for the long voyage ahead. But very little food is carried aboard — only a few barrels of fresh water and sour milk, some flour and bags of dried fish and meat.

Knut and his men will steal what food they need from the villages they raid. They are hoping to find many rich monasteries to rob of their goods and treasures. Between raids, the warriors will camp on shore. But they must stay close to their ships in case they are attacked and have to make a quick get-away. Only Knut has a tent and a proper bed to sleep on. His men must make do with skin sleeping bags and the hard ground.

SEA CHESTS

OARS →

FURS TO
KEEP WARM

FRESH
WATER

FREYDA

SOUR
MILK

BAGS OF
DRIED
MEAT AND
FISH

COOKING THINGS

KNUT'S TENT
AND BED

COLLAPSIBLE
STAND FOR
CAULDRON

CARPENTERS'
TOOLS

BJÖRN

ASTRID

KNUT

ERIC

OIL
LAMP

SVEN

COUSIN
OLAF

ROLLO
GIVES OLAF
HIS NEW
AXE

11

Setting Off

At dawn the next day, the chieftains and their warriors begin the long, hard voyage to Ireland. It is a good day for sailing, with a clear sky and a strong wind behind them.

Knut is excited about spending the summer raiding. But Astrid and the other women are sad to see their men go—some may not return. They may be killed in battle or drowned at sea.

The raiders will spend several days living and sleeping on their ships out of sight of land. It is very cramped on board and they will have an uncomfortable journey with little to do.

COUSIN OLAF

STEERING OAR

Cousin Olaf is helmsman on his ship. As the men row, he guides it down the fjord past dangerous rocks near the shore. By moving the tiller on the steering oar, Olaf can make the ship go left or right. In shallow water, he lifts it clear of the bottom. Each rower sits on a big, wooden chest, packed with his belongings.

FREYDA

Life on Board

Ship life is very boring when the weather is calm and the wind is blowing in the right direction. There is nothing to do but eat, sleep and fish. At night the men sleep on deck in bags made of skin. They take turns to keep watch for land and sleep during the day.

KNUT SAYS GOODBYE TO ASTRID

On this warship the crew now raise the mast and hoist the sail. It is very tricky and heavy work—the mast is long and weighs over 300 kilos. Most of the oars have been pulled in, but a few of the men keep theirs in the water to steady the ship as the mast goes up.

Sailing out of the fjord, the leading ship heads for the open sea. Its big, square sail is lashed to a long pole called the yard-arm which can be turned to catch the wind. The crew use the ropes at the bottom corners of the sail to control it.

Finding the Way

If possible, the Vikings sail along the coasts. But when they sail out of sight of land, they use the sun, the North Star and a kind of compass to help them go in the right direction. Coastal birds show them that land is near.

SEALS

OARS

TILLER

LOG BEING CARRIED TO FRONT OF SHIP

ERIC

Eric is in charge of his father's new warship. Slaves help him and the crew to push it into the water. As the ship moves slowly over the logs, the men pick up those at the back and lay them in front of the ship.

13

Raiding a Monastery

For two days now the raiders have been in Ireland. After one successful raid on a village, they have found a rich monastery to rob of its precious treasures. The younger warriors hope to win fame by fighting bravely, seizing riches and capturing prisoners to take home.

When they saw the Viking warships, the terrified people from nearby farms fled to the walled monastery for safety. They sent a runner off to fetch help. A few men armed themselves with hunting spears and woodmen's axes. The monks hurried into the church and prayed to God to save them from the pagan warriors.

The raiders set fire to the houses to force out the people. Their attack must be quick and they must leave before news of their arrival spreads. As soon as they have seized enough treasure and prisoners, they will sail down the coast to set up camp. There they will share out the loot, dress their wounds, mend their weapons and get ready for another raid.

NOBLEMAN'S FORT

A party of warriors ride off on stolen horses to raid a nearby nobleman's house.

A herdsman tries to drive his sheep away to save them from the raiders.

HERDSMAN

Young monks rush from the burning schoolhouse where they have their daily lessons.

SCHOOL HOUSE

Knut has snatched the treasure from the church. The gold altar cross and gospel book will fetch a good price in Norway. He will give the casket to Astrid as a present.

YOUNG MONKS

BJÖRN

KNUT

MONKS

SVEN

ERIC

Eric and Sven have found a hoard of hidden treasure. When he next goes trading, Sven will sell the silver plates. The coins can be made into fine jewellery.

Irish horsemen attack the Vikings who have been left to guard the ships. Until help arrives, the raiders link their shields together to defend themselves. Cousin Olaf has been badly wounded by an Irish arrow.

IRISH HORSEMEN

COUSIN OLAF

Some raiders slaughter cows and sheep to take back to the camp for roasting. Three others have gone off in search of bread and honey.

A chieftain counts the prisoners herded together against the monastery wall. The abbot will only be released if the Irish pay a ransom to the raiders of a bag of silver. The others will be sold as slaves in Norway.

GRAVE STONE

ARMED VILLAGERS

CHIEFTAIN

THE ABBOT

Three villagers do their best to fight off the attack, killing one Viking with their hunting spears.

A MONK'S HOUSE

Women and children are rounded up by the raiders. They will be taken as slaves. A few lucky ones manage to escape.

15

A Big Feast

At the end of the summer, Knut and his warriors sailed back to Norway. Their ship was loaded with goods and prisoners from many successful raids.

Astrid has prepared a huge feast to celebrate the raiders' victories. For days, she and the women have worked hard cooking a splendid meal. For such a special occasion, cows and sheep have been slaughtered to roast on spits. And deer and wild boars have been hunted in the forest.

Knut invited the other chieftains to the feast. But Cousin Olaf has been taken home. He is gravely ill and Knut fears he may die.

Everyone wears their best clothes and jewellery for the feast. The longhouse rings with their laughter and songs. Each raider brags of his bravery and cunning against the enemy. Long into the night, they drink and talk, telling stories of storms at sea, and the strange land and people they have seen.

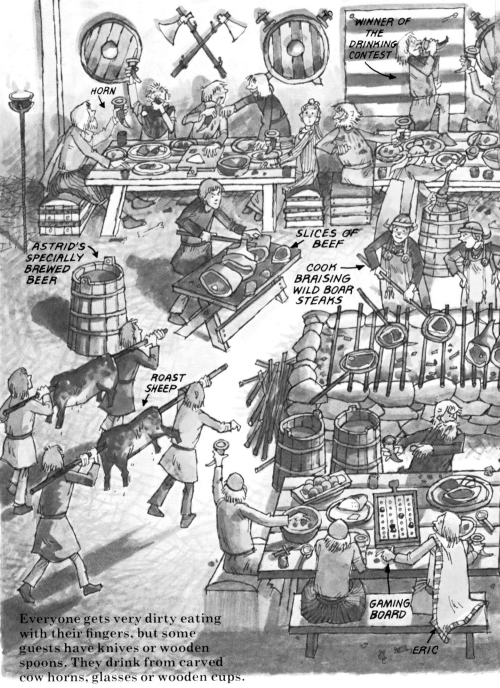

WINNER OF THE DRINKING CONTEST

HORN

ASTRID'S SPECIALLY BREWED BEER

SLICES OF BEEF

COOK BRAISING WILD BOAR STEAKS

ROAST SHEEP

GAMING BOARD

ERIC

Everyone gets very dirty eating with their fingers, but some guests have knives or wooden spoons. They drink from carved cow horns, glasses or wooden cups.

Astrid's Jewellery

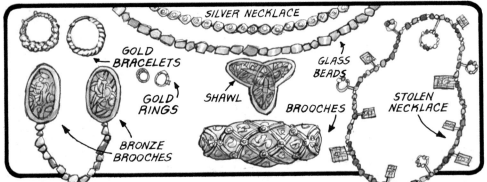

SILVER NECKLACE

GOLD BRACELETS

GOLD RINGS

SHAWL

GLASS BEADS

BROOCHES

STOLEN NECKLACE

BRONZE BROOCHES

Rollo, the blacksmith, has made many fine pieces of jewellery for Astrid. Over the hot charcoals of his fire, he melts down gold coins and silver bowls.

Then he works the precious metals into brooches, necklaces, rings and bracelets. Knut has stolen jewellery on his raids and brought it back for Astrid to wear.

Astrid's Jewel Box

This is Astrid's new jewel box. The words the rune master has carved on it say 'Astridr a Kistu Thasa' which means 'Astrid owns this casket'.

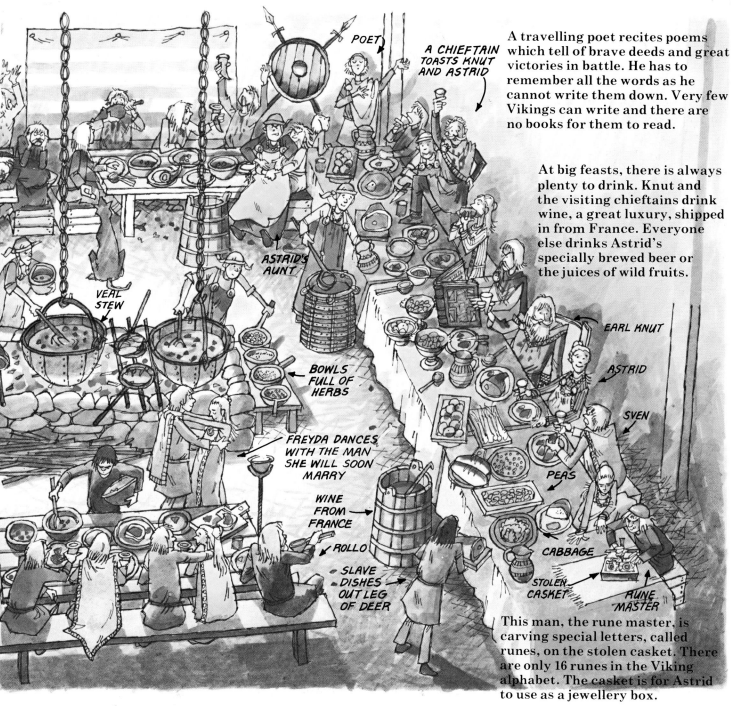

A travelling poet recites poems which tell of brave deeds and great victories in battle. He has to remember all the words as he cannot write them down. Very few Vikings can write and there are no books for them to read.

At big feasts, there is always plenty to drink. Knut and the visiting chieftains drink wine, a great luxury, shipped in from France. Everyone else drinks Astrid's specially brewed beer or the juices of wild fruits.

POET

A CHIEFTAIN TOASTS KNUT AND ASTRID

ASTRID'S AUNT

VEAL STEW

BOWLS FULL OF HERBS

FREYDA DANCES WITH THE MAN SHE WILL SOON MARRY

WINE FROM FRANCE

ROLLO

SLAVE DISHES OUT LEG OF DEER

EARL KNUT

ASTRID

SVEN

PEAS

CABBAGE

STOLEN CASKET

RUNE MASTER

This man, the rune master, is carving special letters, called runes, on the stolen casket. There are only 16 runes in the Viking alphabet. The casket is for Astrid to use as a jewellery box.

How to Cook Meat

Spit-Roasted

First a slave cuts off the head and feet of a dead animal and takes out its insides. Then he roasts the meat over the fire on a long, iron rod.

Baked

HOT STONES

MEAT

Sometimes meat is baked in a big hole in the ground. Hot stones are packed round the meat and it is covered with earth until it is cooked.

1 Boiled

WOOD LINED PIT

HERBS

This way of cooking meat takes a long time. A wood-lined pit is filled with water and chunks of meat are put into it. To make it more tasty, the

2

HOT STONES

cook adds herbs, such as cumin, juniper berries, mustard seeds and garlic. Then she drops hot stones from the fire into the pit to heat the water.

17

Cousin Olaf Dies

Cousin Olaf is dying from his battle wounds. At his bedside, Knut and Astrid pray to the Viking gods to help save the famous chieftain's life.

They believe that their gods are magnificent heroes, who can perform great feats of magic and strength and who are powerful, fearless warriors.

The family beg Thor, god of thunder, and Odin, chief of the gods, to answer their prayers. Without their help and powers, Olaf Strongarm will die.

1 At Olaf's Bedside

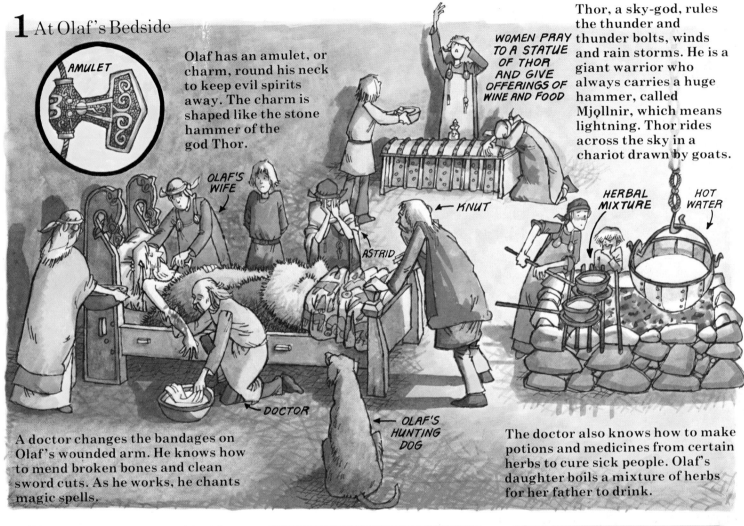

AMULET

Olaf has an amulet, or charm, round his neck to keep evil spirits away. The charm is shaped like the stone hammer of the god Thor.

OLAF'S WIFE

WOMEN PRAY TO A STATUE OF THOR AND GIVE OFFERINGS OF WINE AND FOOD

← KNUT

ASTRID

HERBAL MIXTURE

HOT WATER

Thor, a sky-god, rules the thunder and thunder bolts, winds and rain storms. He is a giant warrior who always carries a huge hammer, called Mjǫllnir, which means lightning. Thor rides across the sky in a chariot drawn by goats.

DOCTOR

← OLAF'S HUNTING DOG

A doctor changes the bandages on Olaf's wounded arm. He knows how to mend broken bones and clean sword cuts. As he works, he chants magic spells.

The doctor also knows how to make potions and medicines from certain herbs to cure sick people. Olaf's daughter boils a mixture of herbs for her father to drink.

2 Prayers and medicine did not save Olaf's life. His grief-stricken wife prepares his body for burial. Olaf will be buried in his best clothes and finest jewellery.

3 Olaf's body is carried to the family cemetery in a horse-drawn wagon. His father, also a great chieftain, and his mother were buried there when they died.

4 Two of Olaf's finest horses and his faithful hunting dog are led away to be killed. By some magic, the people believe, they will live again with Olaf in his after-life.

5 The Burial

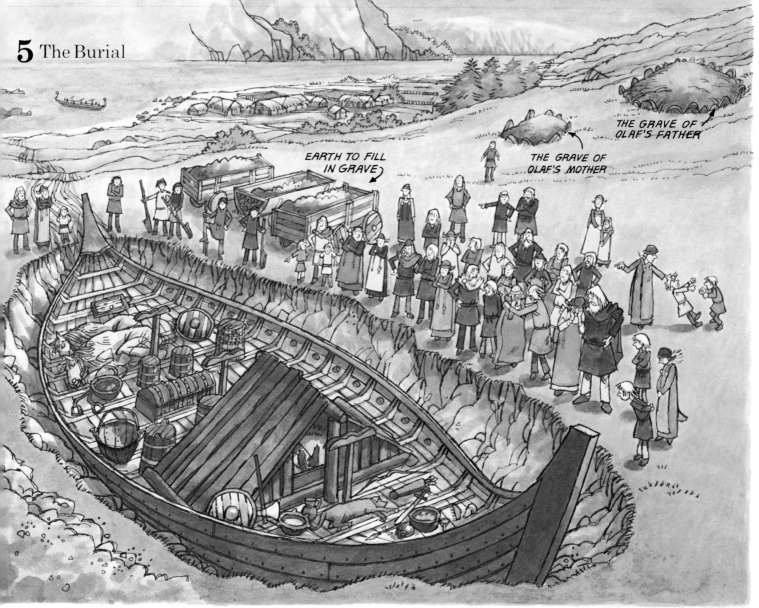

THE GRAVE OF OLAF'S FATHER

THE GRAVE OF OLAF'S MOTHER

EARTH TO FILL IN GRAVE

Because he was such a famous and wealthy man, Cousin Olaf is buried with his warship. A special wooden chamber has been built on the deck for him to lie in.

The Vikings believe that Olaf will sail in his ship to another world. His most treasured and useful possessions are buried with him to help him in this life-after-death.

He will probably live in Valhalla—the Viking heaven. Here the god Odin has a splendid hall for the dead. Only the bravest and greatest warriors go to Valhalla.

How Other Vikings are Buried

Poor Person's Grave

Poor people are buried in a big hole in the ground with a few of their belongings. This Viking woman has two spindles, a comb and a barrel of milk at her side.

Funeral Pyre

Sometimes dead Viking warriors are burnt on a pile of wood called a pyre. Their swords are bent, their spears broken and shields slashed and thrown on the fire with them.

Slave Dies with Master

This slave was killed to be buried with her master. Very few slaves die like this. Because he was a rich farmer, her master has a wood-lined grave.

Björn Sails to Iceland

The following spring, Björn plans to take his family to live in Iceland. Some freemen and a few slaves are going with him to help build a house and work on the land.

In Norway, most of the good land is already being farmed. There is little left for young farmers and their families. Many have left to settle and farm in other countries.

It will take Björn several weeks to reach Iceland. He will sail in the new ship his father has given him. It has a big hold in the deck to carry all the cargo Björn is taking with him.

1 Getting Ready to Leave

BJÖRN →

WEAVING LOOM

PLOUGH

BARLEY SEED

SLEDGE

SOUR MILK AND FRESH WATER

As well as household things, clothes and camping gear, Björn loads animals into the ship for breeding in Iceland. He is taking his plough, food for the animals and bags of barley seed to plant.

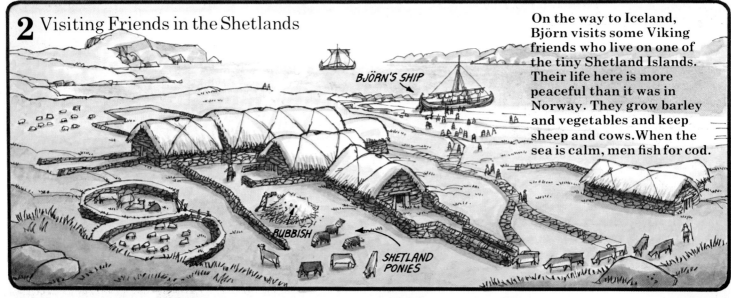

2 Visiting Friends in the Shetlands

On the way to Iceland, Björn visits some Viking friends who live on one of the tiny Shetland Islands. Their life here is more peaceful than it was in Norway. They grow barley and vegetables and keep sheep and cows. When the sea is calm, men fish for cod.

BJÖRN'S SHIP

RUBBISH

SHETLAND PONIES

3 Shipwrecked on the Faroes

Björn and his family stay with their friends for a few days before sailing on. After four calm days at sea, they are caught in a bad storm near the rocky coast of the Faroe Islands.

Björn struggles to keep his ship away from the islands but it is blown on to jagged rocks. Although it is battered by the waves and holed on one side, he and his crew manage to row the ship ashore.

4 Repairing the Ship

Safe on the shore, the friendly islanders help Björn to repair his ship. They left Norway six years ago to settle here. They tell Björn more about Iceland and say there is still plenty of good farming land for new settlers.

5 Arriving in Iceland

When the ship is ready, Björn sets off once again. After many days at sea, he sees Iceland on the horizon. It is a strange island, with plumes of smoke and steam from volcanoes, and jagged, treeless mountains topped with snow.

As he sails round the south coast of the island, Björn finds that all the flat land has already been settled. But further west, he discovers some unclaimed land that looks good for farming. The soil is rich and there is plenty of grass for his animals.

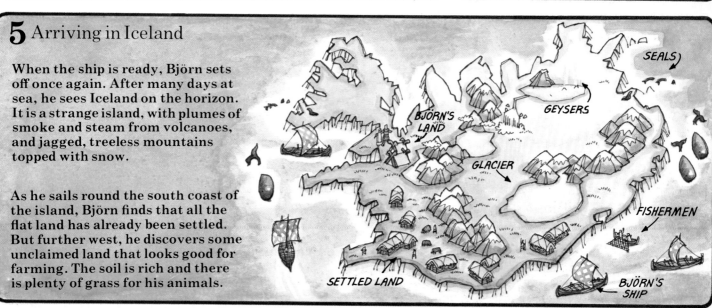

SEALS

GEYSERS

BJÖRN'S LAND

GLACIER

FISHERMEN

SETTLED LAND

BJÖRN'S SHIP

Sven Goes Trading

In autumn, after another summer of raiding, Sven takes his wife down the coast to the big trading town of Hedeby. With his share of the loot—six young, healthy slaves and a bag of silver, Sven hopes to buy silk cloth and other costly things that come from foreign countries. Knut has also given him some soapstone bowls from the farm to sell.

Hedeby is a very exciting place. Today it is full of Viking merchants, busy exchanging their goods.

A few Arab traders have travelled overland from Asia to sell silk and buy slaves to take back home. As the Viking men trade, they joke and tell stories of their recent raids. The women stop to hear the latest gossip and to stare at the strange foreigners.

In many parts of the town, craftsmen are hard at work—making combs, skin shoes and woollen cloth to trade with. Clay pots, amber beads, farm tools, ropes and weapons are on sale as well.

PALISADE TO HARBOUR SHIPS AND KEEP OUT ENEMIES

TRADING SHIPS

FISH

GUARD KEEPS WATCH FOR INVADERS

Sven Buys Wine and Silk

ARAB TRADER SELLING SILK

SOAPSTONE BOWLS

SVEN

BARREL OF WINE

In mid-winter, there will be a festival on Knut's farm. Sven buys wine and drinking glasses for the feast. In exchange, he gives the trader three Irish slaves and silver arm bands. The silver is weighed on scales.

Vikings weigh silver to find out how much it is worth. Arm and neck bands are worth the same as equal weights of coins. Later on, Sven will sell three more slaves and some soapstone bowls to buy silk for his wife.

Most of the houses in Hedeby are made of wattle and daub (sticks woven together and packed with mud). Some are made from split tree trunks. The reed-thatched roofs have a hole in the gables to let out the smoke from the fire.

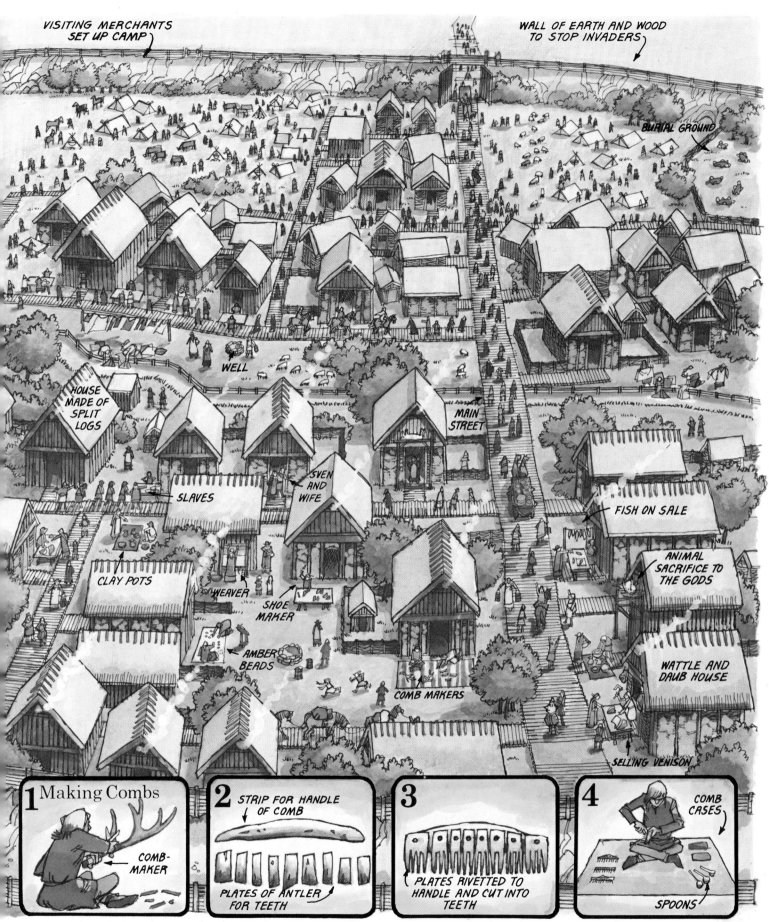

VISITING MERCHANTS SET UP CAMP

WALL OF EARTH AND WOOD TO STOP INVADERS

BURIAL GROUND

WELL

HOUSE MADE OF SPLIT LOGS

MAIN STREET

SVEN AND WIFE

SLAVES

FISH ON SALE

CLAY POTS

WEAVER

SHOE MAKER

AMBER BEADS

ANIMAL SACRIFICE TO THE GODS

WATTLE AND DAUB HOUSE

COMB MAKERS

SELLING VENISON

1 Making Combs

COMB-MAKER

2 STRIP FOR HANDLE OF COMB

PLATES OF ANTLER FOR TEETH

3 PLATES RIVETTED TO HANDLE AND CUT INTO TEETH

4 COMB CASES

SPOONS

The craftsman makes his combs out of deer antlers. First he cuts the points off the antler and shaves down the rough outside.

Then the comb-maker carves a smooth, flat strip to make the top of the comb, and cuts small plates for the teeth.

He rivets the plates to the top and then cuts them up into fine teeth. Then he decorates the comb with carvings.

Craftsmen also make comb cases, spoons, spindles and handles for knives out of bone. They sell them to the traders.

23

Björn Settles in Iceland

Björn and his family have been in Iceland for almost three months. At first they camped while the freemen and slaves built a farmhouse. Now they have all moved in to it.

Autumn in Iceland is a busy time for farmers. Some settlers, who live nearby, have come to help Björn get things ready before the winter begins. They cut the long grass to make into hay, and rake up the fallen leaves. Björn's animals will need a lot of food if they are to live through the long, cold winter.

All summer, his sheep, cows and goats have been grazing in the meadows. Now they must be herded together and driven down to the farm for shelter. Sturdy goats may be let out to graze, but it will be too cold for sheep and cows.

Björn's wife is worried that the family may not have enough food for the winter. She guts fish to dry on racks in the wind. The meat from slaughtered animals is pickled, salted and packed into barrels.

Björn's new farmhouse is built of driftwood washed up on the beach, and cartloads of heavy stones. Thick blocks of turf cover the roof to keep out the cold.

Everyone gathers in the hall to eat, work and chat. Earth is packed into platforms along the walls for them to sit and sleep on. There is also a big living room.

Work in Iceland

1 Salting Meat

CAULDRON OF SEAWATER

Big cauldrons filled with seawater and seaweed are boiled over a wood fire. When all the water boils away, crystals of salt are left on the bottom of the pots.

2

DEAD COW

CRYSTALS OF SALT

One woman scrapes the crystals from the pots, another chops up a dead cow. To stop the meat from going bad, strips are packed in barrels with the salt.

Drying Meat and Fish

While Björn's wife dries chunks of meat and gutted cod, a freeman teaches his son how to light a fire of moss and twigs. He strikes a hard stone against some iron to make the first spark.

HAYSTACK

COLLECTING GRASS

HALL

ANIMALS ARE LED TO SHELTER

ANIMAL BARN

RUBBISH HEAP

BJÖRN'S WIFE

GUTTED FISH

RACKS OF COD AND HERRING

Netting Birds

In spring, thousands of guillemots and puffins make their nests on the ledges of cliffs. Brave men climb carefully up the dangerous rocks to trap the birds in big nets. Today the climb has been successful. The men have caught many birds to eat.

Here the women sit close to the hearth to do their work. They will spend most of the winter spinning and weaving, feeding the animals and looking after the children.

When the winter is over, Björn will plough his field and plant a crop of barley. The family will help him dig up peat and chop up wood for fuel for the summer.

Catching a Whale

Björn spotted this small whale while he was out fishing. He and his crew drive it into shallow water to kill it. The whale blubber will be melted down for oil. The meat is good for eating.

Hunting Seals

Two hunters creep up on seals basking in the sun. They will spear as many as they can before the seals slip back into the sea. Vikings make ropes and shoes from sealskin and eat seal meat.

Collecting Feathers

An eider duck makes her nest on the ground. She plucks down from her breast to line the nest. Two women collect some of the down to fill pillows and bed covers. They also steal some tasty eider eggs.

A Meeting of the Thing

Earl Knut and other freemen from this area of Norway have come to attend a big meeting. This gathering of freemen, which happens a few times a year, is called the Thing.

The men are here to discuss important local business matters, and to decide what to do with three criminals. Some have brought their wives to join in the discussions.

Everyone has set up camp nearby as the Thing will probably last for many days. It is a good opportunity for sports and gossip, and for tinkers to do a bit of trading.

Two criminals are led away to be punished. The man, a thief, is to have one hand cut off. The woman, found guilty of being a witch, will be stoned or drowned.

STALLION

TINKERS

ROLLO'S WIFE

ROLLO'S SON

WITCH

THIEF

LEIF

LAW SPEAKER

EARL KNUT

Knut and Astrid are particularly interested in the meeting. Leif, their apprentice blacksmith, is accused of murdering his master, Rollo, in a fit of rage. Now it will be decided if he is guilty.

The Earl and four local chieftains have been chosen to head the meeting. One of them, the law speaker, recites the law to the crowd. Together they must all agree on Leif's punishment.

Leif, a very stubborn man, refuses to answer any questions. The crowd find him guilty of murder. As a punishment, he is banished from the land. Leif must go at once before Rollo's family kill him.

Weight Lifting

Vikings love to show off their great strength. One of their favourite games is to see who can lift the heaviest boulder. This man is delighted—he has just won the boulder-lifting competition.

Wrestling

Wrestling is also a popular sport. Each day, after the freemen have ended their talks, the toughest Vikings compete against each other to see who is the best and strongest wrestler.

Stallion Fighting

Fierce, wild stallions—specially bred for fighting—have been brought to the Thing. Sometimes, during a horse-fight, the owners get so excited, they start to fight with each other.

A Winter Festival

Tonight, Knut and Astrid have asked all their friends to a festival at the farm. They hold one every winter. Astrid is known throughout the district for her good parties and her delicious food.

The family are very excited. It is always great fun at the feast, with poets and ballad singers, dancing and drinking to entertain the guests.

There is much to do before everyone arrives. Astrid and Freyda prepare the food and drink. Sven collects wood for the hearth. The children are just a nuisance—they much prefer play to work.

WOOD FOR HEARTH

SVEN

STORE HOUSE

ASTRID

KNUT

DRIED MEAT AND FISH

FREYDA

SNOW CLEARED OFF ICE

SPECIALLY BREWED BEER

DEER

ERIC

WOODEN SKIS

BONE SKATES

Eric returns from a successful hunting trip. The four deer he has speared and the snared rabbits will be dished up at the feast tonight.

The Vikings' World

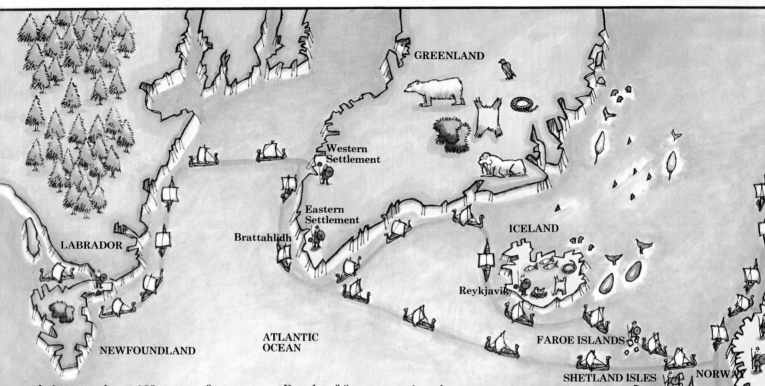

It is now about 100 years after your trip to Norway. Move the place and date dials on your Magic Helmet and look down on the world the Vikings have explored and invaded since then.

They have sailed from their homes in Scandinavia to raid and settle in many towns of Britain and Ireland. There, over the years, they have killed hundreds of people and carried others off as slaves.

Bands of fierce warriors have gone south, down big rivers into Europe and even as far as North Africa to steal, kill and trade. In Central Asia, they have met Arabs, with their long caravans of camels, coming back from China with fine silk and other rare things to sell.

Many Norwegian Vikings have braved the open sea and sailed west to explore and settle in Iceland, Greenland and America.

What the Vikings Found

timber	weapons	jewels	pottery	falcons	Arabs
furs	feathers	wheat	glass	spices	Slavs
walrus ivory	soap-stone	tin	gold	sword blades	Vikings
hides	cloth	honey	amber	Viking overland routes	Franks
ropes	slaves	salt	silver	Viking river routes	caravan routes
fish	loot	wine	silk	Viking sea routes	trading towns

28

ARCTIC OCEAN

As great warriors, adventurers, traders and settlers the Vikings have travelled to many parts of the world. This map shows you the ways they went, all the places they have visited, the people they have met and the things they have found on their travels.

Tashkent

Samarkand

Bulgar

ARAL SEA

Bokhara

Staraja Lagoda

Novgorod

Gnezdovo

SWEDEN

Grobina

Wiskiauten

R. Volga

CASPIAN SEA

Birka

Truso

Kiev

Gurgan

Wolin

R. Dneiper

R. Elbe

Prague   Cracow

Mainz

R. Danube

BLACK SEA

R. Tigris

ITALY

Constantinople

R. Euphrates

Baghdad

PERSIAN GULF

Rome

SARDINIA

Sidon

CRETE

CYPRUS

Jerusalem

SICILY

Alexandria

MEDITERRANEAN SEA

NORTH AFRICA

The Story of the Vikings

The first Viking raids began in about 793 A.D. when a band of Viking warriors attacked the monastery on Lindisfarne, a small island on the north-east coast of Britain. There they murdered many people and captured others. News of this attack spread terror all over Europe. Many Christian people there had already heard of these fierce men from the North.

A year later, the raiders came back to England and attacked monasteries at Monkwearmouth and Jarrow. In 795 A.D., Vikings from Norway began raiding Ireland, killing and looting everywhere they went. About this time, a few Norwegian Vikings settled on the Scottish islands, and on the Isle of Man.

Other bands of Viking raiders sailed in their warships along the coasts of Germany, France, Spain, Italy and North Africa. There they stole whatever riches they could find, again killing people and taking others as slaves.

Swedish Vikings went east to Russia, sailing down the great Volga and Dneiper rivers to raid and settle in towns such as Staraja Ladoga, Kiev, Novgorod and Gnezdovo.

At this time, the Vikings worshipped their own gods, like Thor, Odin and Frey. A missionary monk, called St. Ansgar, went to Birka in 830 to try to convert the people to Christianity. But he did not have much success. It was a long time before the Vikings became Christians.

From 835 A.D. onwards raids on England and Ireland became more and more frequent. Instead of making hit-and-run raids, as they had done before, the Northmen set up camps and stayed during the winter months. Then they began raiding again in the spring and summer. In 841, they settled for the first time in Ireland, at Dublin.

By now, many Vikings were leaving their homes to settle in other countries. In 860, Norwegian explorers discovered Iceland. The first Viking farmers settled there ten years later. By 930, about 10,000 Vikings were living there. The first Althing, a parliament, met and created a new Icelandic republic.

In 867, Danish raiders in England captured the city of York. Soon they had settled all over Northumbria. After years of battle between the Danes and the English, King Alfred of England signed a treaty with the Danish leader Guthrum. They divided the country between them. The Danish part of England was known as the Danelaw.

This treaty did not bring peace. The Vikings continued to raid the English coasts and King Alfred had to defend his land in many battles. It was not until 926, when Aethelstan was king, that the English recaptured Northumbria from the Danes. Aethelstan gathered a huge army and defeated them in a great battle.

Early in the 10th century, bands of Vikings sailed from Ireland to north-west England. They fought many battles, overpowering the people who lived there. Many Vikings also settled in northern Scotland. In Ireland—Dublin and Limerick became important trading ports.

In 911, Rollo, a Danish leader, took his warriors to Normandy in France. There they captured land from the Franks. Their leader, Charles the Simple, signed a treaty with Rollo making Normandy Viking territory.

It was not until about 930 that the Danish Vikings started to become Christians. Their king, Harald Bluetooth, was converted ten years later. In Norway, the people were forced to adopt the Christian religion. But many of them still continued to worship their own gods.

A Norwegian Viking, Eric the Red, who had been banished to Iceland for killing a man, heard of an unexplored island. In 982, he sailed from Iceland to live on this island which he called Greenland. A few years later he returned to Iceland with news of Greenland. Many people went back with him to live there.

In 1002, Erik's son, Leif Eriksson, sailed west from Greenland and found an island which he called 'Vinland'. This was probably Newfoundland. America had been discovered about 15 years before by a Viking explorer who had been blown off-course trying to get to Greenland. Some Vikings followed Leif to live in Vinland.

Early in the 11th century, the English were forced to pay money to the Vikings to make them leave their towns and people in peace. For several years the Vikings were given many pounds of silver to go away. This money was called Danegeld. But they kept returning until in 1016, Canute, king of Denmark, invaded and became king of England.

During this time, the Norwegian Vikings finally became Christians. They built churches to worship in and set up stones, called runestones, in memory of people who had died. The stones were carved with the runic alphabet (Viking alphabet) and many different patterns. But it was not until the 12th century that the Swedish Vikings finally became Christians.

Christianity changed the Vikings' way of life. They were not so fierce and no longer made many raids or demanded Danegeld. By 1066, the raids ceased and the Vikings settled down to a much quieter, more peaceful life. But they were still great traders and continued to trade in Britain and Ireland and all over Europe.

Wherever the Vikings settled they adopted the language and customs of the people there. They soon became French, English, Russian, Scots, or Irish themselves. Later, the people in Scandinavia, the Vikings' homeland, became Norwegians, Swedes and Danes. Even today, in the countries in which they settled, you can see the descendants of the tall, blond and blue-eyed Vikings.

Index

Further Reading

The Vikings and their Origins
  By David M. Wilson (Thames and Hudson)

The Vikings by Michael Gibson
  (Wayland Ltd.)

Vikings and Norsemen by
  Bernard Henry (John Baker Ltd.)

First published in 1977 by
Usborne Publishing Ltd
Usborne House
83-85 Saffron Hill
London EC1N 8RT, England.

Copyright © 1990, 1977 Usborne
Publishing Ltd.

Printed in Belgium

The name Usborne and the device
are Trade Marks of Usborne Publishing Ltd.